From a Lover's Mouth

A collection of poetry

Whitney Cason

DEDICATION

This is dedicated to all those who have put their entire soul into the complexities of love. To those who have gained, lost, wanted and regretted love in any way; these words are for all of us.

Un

Love Is

Love has the ability to grab ahold of your soul; take every ounce of energy you have and leave you drained and confused.

Love is a fight and sometimes you get knocked out; and sometimes no one wins. Sometimes love is a war and when you choose to fight, you risk leaving your life on the battlefield.

Love is waking up with the glow of morning and your soulmate is lying there next you; and you realize that glow is their smile.

I thought love was sunshine on a cloudy day, when really love is weathering the storm and finding the light at the end of the tunnel.

Love lies because sometimes the truth is too much of a burden to bear.

Love is knowing when to say you've had enough torture and resent how much hell you put yourself through being in it.

In all the pains and all the pleasures, love can be God's greatest gift.

Love Me before The Sunrise

I know it's wrong, and I may regret it in a few hours, but I just want you to love me until the sunrise.

I know I shouldn't want this anymore, because we are no longer one. We both understood that love was a road we would only travel together.

You weren't ready for the commitment and I was not ready to fight you for it. I loved you enough to let you go, but now I long for any moment in time where you would treat me like you used to.

Hold me close and inhale my scent. Whisper sweet nothings in my ear about how I'm the best thing that has happened to you, and how much I make you happy.

I want to tell you how much joy you bring to me and that I never want this feeling to end; even if it's only true until the sunrise.

I know that when the sunrise comes, we will part ways, and reality will set in. We won't be lovers, but we agreed to be friends. As much as it hurts, I know it is the only way I can keep a connection with you.

Clearly, desires of my flesh made me send that text; and now here we are, lying sweaty and exhausted between your sheets.

I wish you would put your arm around me, kiss me on my forehead, and make me feel wanted. I hope you can make me feel like I never made the mistake of wanting you.

It sounds desperate, stupid, and I'm the worst love-struck puppy there is...but all I want is for you to love me before the sunrise. At least one last time.

I'll try to be content with that...

Blessing

Yesterday I had a talk with you; and my soul opened up and the sun shined brighter once it realized a transformation had begun.

My heart sang out with a feeling of content and joy injected itself into my veins and invaded my body like a drug.

Tears fell from my eyes and a smile appeared on my face like the sun emerging after a violent storm.

I guess this is what a blessing feels like.

Crave

Can I trace love notes on your inner thigh, while I whisper how much I love you in your ear?

Can I look you in the eye, so you can see how deep the fire runs for you?

I crave so many pieces of you until they become whole; a nibble on your ear lobe, nuzzling the place where your neck and collarbone connect, leaving traces of my kisses softly on your lips.

Craving you has become a routine, the thoughts of loving you have kept me satisfied...

But my fear is I will never lose track of you...

And this craving will become a nagging pain in my heart, something that will never get completely fulfilled.

My mind fights with the reasoning behind my hesitation for you, but my soul continues to yearn for a moment in time where it all becomes so perfect.

The Thought of Being in Love

Instead of being in love with the idea of being in love, I want to be in love with the idea of being in love with you.

In love with the idea of never being held by anyone else; or touched by anyone else, or kissed by anyone else but you.

I want to be in love with the idea of waking up next to you and watching the way you are comforted by my presence.

How you sleep soundly knowing you can feel my lips on the back of your neck,

Or how you curl into me whenever you feel me grab your waist.

I want to be in love with the idea of seeing your smile every day and how it lights up even the darkest parts of my existence,

How it warms even the coldest parts of my heart; the parts that I didn't know could feel that warmth again.

I want to be in love with the idea of anticipating your next word, or having the same thought at the same time.

We are so in sync with each other mentally and emotionally that in the places you begin, I end.

I'm in love with the thought of being in love, but I'm more in love with the thought of being in love with you.

Magnetic Fate

The moment was something like a movie.

From the moment we met, the world around us stopped.

You had the ability to stop time around us so that we could revel in the moment that we made eye contact.

We moved to the rhythm of our own love song; soulful, yet full of insecurity and doubt, not fully confident that this would even work out.

Despite our hesitation, we could not hide the fact that we were drawn to the idea of us becoming one.

With a world full of souls to love, ours picked each other, as if there were magnets in our chests that were made to slowly bring us together.

Daydream

Words escape me as you pass me by.

I try to speak, but my words are halted by the speed bump in my throat as you slide through my peripheral vision..

See, I felt something instant even in the distance because our eyes made a connection that radiated through every nerve in my body.

Immediate fantasies of those same eyes roaming my body.

Allowing your fingertips to paint a portrait on me.

Let the world view what we've created.

Without hesitation I let my thoughts race to forbidden territories involving me and you developing intellectual conversations.

Not thinking of the devastation that would arise if our trance was broken.

This is no joke I'm in fact enveloped in the thoughts of loving you, adoring you.

Touching you, kissing you, making love to you.

Then I'm back to reality and you have vanished from my mental and physically, your presence is a mystery.

Love Unconditional

Before I close my eyes at night, I tell God about you.

I tell Him how I saw Him in you,

I saw that you and Him were one,

And at that moment, I knew that true love was real.

Deux

Mind Game

We can't keep playing these games, baby.

Every night, we sit here, wondering when the foolishness is going to end;

Sporadically making eye contact, but looking away like we are secret crushes sitting two rows away from each other in fifth period math class.

I don't know why we keep playing these games, but one of us needs to make the first move.

Neither one of us want to surrender to the invisible war being fought between our mouths; you know, the one with the unwritten rule that whoever speaks first, shows weakness.

Whoever shows affection first wasn't ever really mad in the first place. It's a constant race and battle to see who can be mad best.

I want to win, but I can't stop thinking about how euphoric it is to lay upon your chest at night.

When the air flows through our bedroom window like water, I can lay underneath your arm; burrowing my face into the hair on your chest and feel your energy transfer through our skin.

And just to lay within your space is a fantasy. To smell that body wash you use makes the heat rise in undisclosed locations bound by locks that only you have been allowed the key to.

I want to give in, to tell you "baby, let's quit this foolishness and engage in some marital extracurricular activities", but I've got a battle to fight and a war to win and my mind says it wouldn't be right to give in.

Let him give in first, because he knows you were right.

But.....what if he doesn't?

Void

Two lovers,

Connected at the hips.

Dancing to the rhythm of staccato breaths and whispered moans

Twist-tying themselves between the silk bed sheets

She; hoping this rendezvous of bodies means that he may actually have feelings for her.

He; trying to drown his sorrows of a lost lover in between the legs of another.

Both not really knowing if this will mean anything in the morning; that is, if they even rise to see the sunset within each other's company.

But for this moment in time, they have found comfort in lust, because neither one of them knows if they were in it for love.

This was only a meeting with the commitment of good sex and a hours away from their respective realities.

When he sits at home wondering if she will call and say he can have another chance,

Or when she comes to grips with the truth that men only want her physically and never challenge her mind,

They both know that time is of the essence, so they entertain each other in fantasy.

So, when this meeting comes to a close there should be no lingering; no awkward pause, no struggle for small talk.

Just a smile and a handshake, and the agreement to meet again the same time next week

Until she realizes he didn't catch feelings; or until he gets over his heartbreak...

Whichever comes first.

The Love Note I'll Never Send

My only wish is that we lived in a world where the possibility of me loving you was reality…

Instead, I hide behind the words I write, pieced together like the harmonies of a love note I will never send.

Your presence radiates and illuminates the darkest tunnels of my heart, reminding me that being madly and intensely in love will always be possible.

I've never been so afraid to love a soul, until I found myself basking in the beauty of yours.

I can barely look into your eyes because they hold a depth I have never seen.

I'm afraid to expose this truth to you, so I hide behind this love note, in hopes that one day my words can tell the story my lips never can.

But will I ever have the courage to open up that door?

Do I have the strength to pour my heart into something with you, or will these words sit merely in the draft of my notebook, never having the chance to be seen for what they are?

I'm mesmerized at just how beautiful your soul is. In a world so dark, with people so dull; your heart shines brighter than the sun in spring.

Most times, the most descriptive words escape me, as I try to make sense of these emotions.

I sit around, fumbling with the perfect string of words to express my desire to have you

But more importantly, the seriousness of how much I need you and this love, in this space and in this time in my life.

Addicted

On nights like this I watch the minutes on the clock.

Counting each one and wondering when you will come back to me.

But deep down, I want you to take all your things and leave the key to my heart on the nightstand on your way out.

My heart yearns for your touch, and I'm a slave to your love; but your inconsistencies and insecurities are things I can see from a mile away.

I hate that you piss me off in one breath, then have me melting at your feet in the next.

I can't get enough of you when I really should be through with you.

On the days when I want to call it quits, I push you away but you find a way back in; you tell me the things I want to hear; the right words, the slightest touch and suddenly, I forgot why I was mad again.

You've found a way to slither back into my garden and wreak havoc on my heart again.

I know I shouldn't let you in but the way you love me is the only love I know.

So, you find a way to fight another day with my heart; playing games with my mind and have me thinking you want all of me, when really all you want to do is pull at my strings.

You like to play puppeteer with the pieces of me, but instead of making this love feel real, you continue to toy with me.

You know my heart goes through withdrawals when you're not around for so long, so when you leave, you wait just long enough before the longing and the temptations begin.

You know me so well, and you know just how long to wait before I'm vulnerable enough to fall victim to your tricks again; you insist on sending me messages; the ones I decline only to hide the fact that I miss you and it's too painful to admit.

I remember the times you dialed my phone and leave voicemails because you know I'll listen to it if it means hearing your voice again, no matter how much I try to resist.

You do all these things to me, knowing at some point I'll succumb to your advances.

You know that even though you ruined me, there's a piece of my heart that you know you still belong in.

You know I have a problem and all you do is feed the flame.

I'm addicted to the worst drug of its kind; loving a man who doesn't deserve the pleasure of loving all of me, and you don't mind being my dealer.

Lover or Friend?

A choice I had to make;

As I looked into the eyes of my lover and my friend.

I knew I couldn't begin to comprehend the predicament I was in.

To choose one over another would require a commitment.

I would have to hold on to one of you as I let the other fade away.

No second thoughts, doubts, regrets or resentment.

We would vow to live in the epitome of contentment.

A choice I had to make between my lover and my friend.

A choice that creates a beginning and an end.

My mind has traveled back and forth for what seems like an eternity.

A battle of the heart and mind; certainty or uncertainty.

If the wrong decision is made, does my heart have the ability to mend?

If the right decision is made, it will give love an opportunity to transcend?

I look into your eyes, unable to decide if I should take your side as lover….or friend…?

Night of Empty Thoughts

Another night lying in bed, searching the ceiling for an answer it didn't have.

Another night of talking to herself, asking questions with no answer.

Another night of empty and idle thoughts. She wondered how perfection felt; wondered what joy was and if happiness ever existed.

She looked over her bed and found him lying there, sleep taking over and rendering him lifeless for the night hours.

He slept, while she suffered, and she felt so helpless.

Her words were never understood, her opinion deemed insignificant; her desires weren't acceptable.

She tried countless times to just let well enough alone, but well enough wasn't what she felt she deserved.

She wanted a love that went above and beyond, one she could lay her life on the line for, one that she could sacrifice herself to be a part of something bigger.

She couldn't see that with him.

As he lay in bed, peacefully sleeping, her eyes kept shifting. She couldn't find rest, couldn't fall into slumber. "what if" kept replaying in her mind in a million different ways.

Seems as though empty thoughts would keep her up another night.

Thoughts so heavy with emotion, anger, disappointment....

And in the morning, the worth of those thoughts would amount to nothing.

Naked Truth

A bare face and a pure soul,

I ask nothing more but for you to see me.

I know this is new to you, something that you may not be used to,

but I had a feeling that between all of the good vibes losing time in each other's eyes, I lied to you.

I didn't mean to and please believe me when I say it was never my plan to lead you on,

But before you profess to me that you have found your forbidden love let me show you me.

Let me show you the woman who puts on the mask of confidence but cries when no one can hear the pain in her.

Let me introduce you to a woman who hides behind a facade of happiness but is slowly dying inside.

I need you to see me for what I'm worth to you, completely bare; with no place to hide the insecurities, so you can tell me if you're really all in.

Don't tell me you love me now, and shy away when the shit gets real.

Don't tell me you're there for me and you're not around when I need someone to wipe my tears.

When the depression starts to eat away at my smile, will I still be the most beautiful woman you have ever seen.

When you find out I've been places and done things, will I still be the woman in your dreams?

Are you ready to know the shit my heart has been through?

Will you stand beneath the storm clouds with me, when the sunlight is too far gone to see?

Will you accept my truth; when it's unclothed and exposed for the world to view?

When my true colors show, will you still want what's left of me?

The parts that don't shine as brightly as you'd like,

The pieces of me that you thought weren't used,

The layers of my soul that have been abused?

Will you still love me if I showed you my naked truth?

Take a minute to think about this, because I need to know if you will still be all in.

Trois

Untitled

I woke up with remnants of our last conversation on the tips of my tongue.

Realizing it wasn't much like conversation, but more like tongue lashing.

Arguing until the sun came up like stars who weren't ready to let the night go so soon.

You said things and then I said things; unholy things, more like things I wouldn't want to repeat to another soul, but our passion and deep rooted insecurities were shown last night.

No one wanted to surrender, but both wanted to be right when we know someone was wrong but I'm still not going to say it was me...

We both fought a war of love last night; I took every punch you threw at me and countered with as much force as I could muster.

In the end, I still managed to stand against the force of your abuse; but we still didn't were just as worse as we started.

So where does it go from here?

When You Came to Get Your Things

It was a cold moment.

In our house, our bedroom. A stare down commenced once you crossed into my sanctuary.

Eyes filled with anger while my heart filled with longing; I maintained a poker face when you came.

Your things were placed neatly in a box, all the things that made me think of you:

The t-shirt I slept in, my favorite cologne; the one that penetrated our space whenever you wore it. Even the painting that hung over our bed that you had custom made for me.....

All these things were reminiscent of you and I want nothing to do with them any longer.

No words were said as you gathered these things, no last minute plea for loves forgiveness and kind heart.

No dialogue of how apologetic you are and your God's honest promise to make it up to me.

I've heard that song sung a million times, and I was too damn tired for a million and one.

I let you back in out of the cold every time; you would nuzzle your way back into my heart and I would give you another chance.

But I've found my breaking point, and I've found that happiness doesn't have to come second to heartbreak.

Heartbreak and betrayal have always served as a prerequisite to your love and affection.

So you take these things, and go back to your doghouse, where you can entertain as many women as you please.

Slave for You

I asked myself if this was really love; or was this painful torture from someone who's supposed to love me.

As time passed, I struggled to find the difference.

I opted for the latter, because anyone who is for the former, wouldn't cause this level of agony.

I lay in bed with you, clutching the sheets as if they held my last shred of sanity and dignity.

I don't want to be a victim of yet another emotional beating and physical pounding, following by what you have considered love making, but what I consider a painstaking assault.

As I lay there underneath you, holding on to any shred of light, I wonder how can you want to place a seed in a vessel you intend to destroy?

You act unbothered, as if these actions are of second nature to you.

When you look in the mirror, is this really what love looks like for you?

When you look at me, do you see the woman you pledged your life to protect, or the rag doll you consider me to be?

I see the venom on the tip of your lips ready to poison what's left of me.

I hate that I gave enough energy to loving you so much that I hate you at the same time.

The End

There is more to life than one word text replies and tear-soaked pillow cases.

I will not let myself believe that I was less of a woman for you.

I'd rather believe that you weren't man enough to handle my magic.

You couldn't comprehend the language my hips spoke or how my tongue cracked your ignorance like a whip.

I was too much woman for you, so you decided to hurt me before you could inevitably feel ashamed to think you could keep a woman like me.

These tears are not filled with pain; but rather laced with the joy of the weight of an exhausting dance with your male ego being lifted off my shoulders.

Thank you for the ride, but it's best that we end this now.

You

I think of you when I should be thinking of myself.

I love you when I should be loving myself.

I breathe life into your soul, while I watch mine wither and die.

I smile for you, when I really want to curl into a ball and cry.

I listen to you, disobeying the words of my inner voice.

I sacrifice for you, feeling as if my soul doesn't have any other choice.

My life I gave to you, no matter what pain came about.

I lived in you, and now I want out.

When Your Love Wasn't Enough

I spent so much time looking for love in all of your places.

Tried to find your emotions between stoic text conversations and late night sessions between the sheets,

I wanted you to adore me, as much as I threw myself into the attention you paid me for just that moment in time.

That time you told me I was the only girl you had eyes for, even while managing to stare intently at every other woman in the room,

I still believed that what you said was the gospel that solidified our union.

I figured, he could look at other girls, because I know that he only will come home to me.

I knew that even though you didn't answer every time I called, or no matter how much I suspected that you were only answering every third time I called; eventually, you answered for me.

I let you treat me less than average, and made myself believe that it was more than enough to meet my needs.

But one day, when I got tired of not hearing your voice; or when I grew weary of feeling the space on your side of the bed empty from where you should lay your head at night,

I started to wonder if your love was enough.

I didn't know how to love myself, so I looked for you to love me enough for the both of us; and I found that it wasn't enough.

I found that there were some things that you couldn't do for me, and I couldn't rely on you to love me, while I worked overtime loving you.

When I finally looked within myself, and noticed there wasn't enough love for myself there, that is when I decided that you were no longer needed to fulfill me

The Walls Around Us

If the walls around us could talk, there'd be a monologue dedicated to us,

About how what once lit a flame for our love is now nothing more than slowly burning embers of what used to be,

You see, we used to be inseparable; our souls connected like jigsaw puzzles

But maybe, baby, somewhere down the line the pieces got mixed up and now nothing fits anymore...

Nothing feels like heaven and it's not quite hell it's just some bullshit in the middle that we don't really want to admit as just being life.

I wanted to fight for the right to love you forever, but I don't know if whatever's at the finish line is worth the battle at the start.

I want to go, but you have padlocked my heart...

The key is lost amongst our memories because I thought I'd never want this love to end.

If the walls around us could talk, I swear they'd have so much to tell,
They would bear the secrets that we promised never to tell a soul,

The good, better and best times; along with the bad and worst times of our lives.

I don't want to end this love without acknowledging how much of a blessing you were to my life.

And like all things, time and growth allowed us to stretch past ourselves and realize that we needed more than what we could give to each other.

Our unfinished disagreements turned into broken promises, that neither were committed to in the first place.

Tensions so thick neither one of us can breathe;

Egos so big, they fill the room to the point of discomfort.

If the walls around us could talk, they'd beg us to stay around,

They would ask us to not give up so soon, and to see if there is some way we can make this life worth living together.

The problem is, we've seen too much, heard too much and experienced too much pain to even know what the happiness feels like anymore...

You Don't Deserve

You don't deserve to be poisoned by my coldness.

You don't deserve to be trapped in a life that's hollow.

You don't deserve to receive what my heart is only capable enough to give right now.

I've outgrown my ability to be worth your love...I don't deserve you, and you don't deserve who I've become.

ABOUT THE AUTHOR

Whitney Cason is a writer and author of her first published novel, Playing with Fire; which debuted April 2016. She currently runs a personal blog, Write, Live and Love. She is currently in the social work field, and enjoys writing and spending time with her family. This is her second published work; and her first published individual collection of poetry.

www.ingramcontent.com/pod-product-compliance
Lightning Source LLC
Chambersburg PA
CBHW071226130626
46555CB00004B/1867